C · L · A · S · S · I · C
AMERICAN FOLK TALES

Retold by Steven Zorn

WITH ILLUSTRATIONS BY GARY GIANNI ★ BRYAN HAYNES

CHET JEZIERSKI ★ STEVE PIETZSCH ★ PAUL SELWYN ★ DAVID SLONIM

RAYMOND SMITH ★ KEN SPENGLER

Produced by Ariel Books

COURAGE BOOKS

AN IMPRINT OF RUNNING PRESS
PHILADELPHIA · LONDON

9 8 7

Digit on the right indicates the number of this printing.

Library of Congress Cataloging-in-Publication Number
91-58125

ISBN 1-56138-062-8

Printed in China
Designed by Michael Hortens
Art direction by Michael Hortens

Published by Courage Books, an imprint of
Running Press Book Publishers, 125 South Twenty-second Street
Philadelphia, Pennsylvania 19103.

Contents

Paul Bunyan
Illustrated by Bryan Haynes 11

Johnny Appleseed
Illustrated by Steve Pietzsch. 16

How Brer Rabbit Tricked Brer Fox
Illustrated by David Slonim 20

John Henry
Illustrated by Ken Spengler 24

Davy Crockett
Illustrated by Gary Gianni 32

The Story of Bobcat & Coyote
Illustrated by Raymond Smith. 40

Pocahontas
Illustrated by Chet Jezierski. 44

Pecos Bill
Illustrated by Paul Selwyn 52

Introduction

Folk tales are the stories a nation tells about itself. These American stories of adventure, humor, bravery, and magic are heard from the northern woods of Maine to the prairies and grasslands of Texas.

Meet the characters—real and imaginary—who helped shape the country, including America's first super-heroes, Paul Bunyan and Pecos Bill. Their larger-than-life adventures led to the lumber and ranching industries. You'll also meet the famous steel-driving man, John Henry. He pitted himself against a steam drill in the early days of the railroad.

The feats of some real-life heroes are just as remarkable as these tall-tale legends. Here's the story of the Indian princess, Pocahontas, whose compassion helped the English settlers in Virginia; the outspoken frontiersman, Davy Crockett; and the peace-loving, tree-planting pioneer, Johnny Appleseed.

To round out our treasury are two tales of crafty animals. Our tale of Coyote, the trickster spirit, comes from the Native Americans of the Great Plains. Brer Rabbit and his friends live on in tales once told by African-Americans.

Each story in this treasury is a colorful piece of a gigantic patchwork quilt. Stitched together, these folktales create a magnificent picture of our nation's heritage.

Steven Zorn

Paul Bunyan

It was a miraculous year in Maine. It began with the usual snowstorm, but the winter wind blew the snow from the roads and stacked it into neat piles along the sides. That spring, rain never fell on the weekends. Whenever the rain did fall, fish and lobsters were caught in the puddles left behind. The cows gave chocolate milk, every egg had two yolks, and the apples and potatoes grew as big as pumpkins. In the summer of that year, Paul Bunyan was born. That was the most surprising thing of all.

From the time he woke up at dawn to the minute his father tucked him in at night, baby Paul did nothing but eat and eat and eat. He would sleep for only a couple of hours, then wake up hungrier than ever. The more he ate, the more he grew, and the more he grew, the more food he needed. The funny thing was, Paul didn't get fatter, he just got bigger and stronger.

He was a clever boy, too. When he was only a few weeks old, he chopped the legs off his father's bed without waking him. The next morning, when his father saw what Paul had done, he beamed with pride. "He's gonna be an excellent woodsman some day," he thought.

Because Paul grew so quickly, Mr. Bunyan had to build a new cradle for him every two days. At the end of three months, Paul was bigger than his father, and he was still growing.

"We've got to do something about the boy, Ma," said Mr. Bunyan to his wife. "Every time he crawls around, he breaks something. There's just no room for him in this house."

"He's just full of spirit, Pa," replied Mrs. Bunyan. "Why don't we convert the barn into a nursery for him? There's plenty of room in there."

The barn made a comfortable nursery for Paul, at least until his feet poked through the barn door and his head bumped against the hayloft. The real problem was getting Paul to fall asleep. Babies like to be rocked to sleep, and Paul, despite his size, was still a baby. But he was too heavy to rock.

After many sleepless nights, Paul's father thought of a solution. He hired a team of horses to haul Paul and his cradle into the Atlantic Ocean, where the waves would lull the baby to sleep. But Paul's wiggling in the huge cradle created tidal waves that threatened the whole coast of Maine. The neighbors were furious. They suggested that the Bunyan family move to Michigan where there was more land—and fewer people to irritate.

So Paul grew up in the Michigan woods. With one swipe of his axe, Paul was able to cut down trees that would take ten ordinary men a week to topple. Word of this mighty lumberjack spread far and wide, and soon Paul Bunyan became the head of a very successful logging crew.

Paul wasn't just big—he was smart, too. He figured that cutting down one tree at a time wasn't the most efficient way to get lumber. So he invented the two-handled saw.

The two-handled saw was more than a mile long. It had jagged teeth in the middle and a handle on each end. Paul would hold one handle, and ten men would hold the other. Each side would take turns pulling the saw, which would cut through a whole grove of trees all at once. The sound of all the falling trees was deafening!

Cutting the trees was only half the job. The hard part was hauling them to the river so they could be sent to the lumber mill. For this job, Paul depended on his best friend: Babe, the blue ox.

Paul had found Babe during the Winter of the Blue Snow. The snow, which was the prettiest shade of blue you ever saw, had been falling for a week. Paul had gone out for a walk when he came upon a little ox calf almost covered by the snow. The calf was a tiny snip of a thing, and blue from the cold.

"Why, you're just a babe," said Paul as he slipped it into his pocket for warmth. "If you live, I'll call you Babe."

Paul carried Babe to the bunkhouse, where he fed him milk and hot-cake crumbs. Babe grew bigger and stronger, but he never lost that blue color. In fact, he turned a deeper shade.

Babe grew at an alarming rate. It took forty two and one-half ax-handles, laid end-to-end, to span the distance between his horns. Babe would eat hundreds of hotcakes each morning, and if he didn't get enough, he would eat the dishes, too. He loved to sneak up behind Paul and butt. Then they would wrestle. Some folks say the Great Lakes are the imprints left by Paul's elbows and Babe's hooves as they frolicked.

Paul built a leather harness so Babe could haul timber to the river. Once it began to rain while Babe was carrying a load of logs. When Babe arrived at the river, the logs were nowhere to be seen. The wet leather had stretched two miles into the woods. Later, when the sun came out, the harness shrank and the logs caught up with the blue ox.

Perhaps Babe's hardest chore was straightening out a logging road. The road was so twisted and winding that the lumberjacks would pass themselves returning from work! Paul yoked Babe to the end of the road and had him pull all the curves out. This saved the loggers considerable travel time.

Paul Bunyan had so many men working for him that he had to build a high-rise bunkhouse for them to sleep in. This bunkhouse was so tall that the top seventeen bunks had hinges on them to let the moon pass by. The men had to ride hot-air balloons to these bunks at night, and use parachutes to come down for breakfast.

What mighty breakfasts the lumberjacks ate! Paul hired Sourdough Sam to make hotcakes for all the men. It wasn't an easy job. Each lumberjack ate a hundred hotcakes, and there were too many men to count. The batter had to be mixed in a concrete mixer, which Paul invented just for this purpose. The skillet was so big that greasing it required three men to skate on it with slabs of bacon tied to their feet.

Sam could always be depended on to find some delicacy to treat the men. He invented pea soup when a wagonload of peas was accidentally dumped into a hot spring.

One time when Paul and his crew were logging in South Dakota, Paul was experimenting with new farming techniques to grow more food for the men. He planted a kernel of corn which sprung six feet overnight and grew a foot a minute all the next day.

Thinking that it was growing too fast to do anyone any good, Paul sent one of his men, a lumberjack named Joe, up the stalk to cut the top. But the stalk grew faster than Joe could climb it. Soon both disappeared into the clouds. And since the stalk was growing at the bottom and the top, Joe couldn't climb down fast enough to ever reach the ground. Paul had to load biscuits into his rifle and fire them up to Joe so he wouldn't starve.

After a couple of days, the corn must've grown too close to the sun, because around noon time, a blizzard of popcorn covered the countryside. A herd of cattle, thinking it was snow, immediately froze to death. The rancher who owned these cows was furious, but Paul offered to buy every head. Sourdough Sam made steaks that night. The cornstalk stopped growing, and it took Joe a week to climb down.

Around this time, Paul received a letter from the king of Sweden. The king said that Sweden was too crowded, and asked if Paul could use some Swedish lumberjacks. Paul replied immediately, telling the king to send as many men as he wished—there were plenty of trees in Minnesota and the Dakotas to be chopped.

Thousands of Swedes came to America, and in no time the trees were cleared from those states. Paul personally pounded every last stump into the ground with his fists, so if you go to Minnesota today, you'll see nothing but prairie.

Johnny Appleseed

Some folks become heroes through bravery. Some folks make their name by being smart or clever. And others are famous for their kindness. Johnny Appleseed had all these qualities, but above all he was kind. He lived his life to help others.

Johnny's real name was John Chapman. He was born near Boston around the year 1775. He was a deeply religious man who always carried the Bible with him. When he was a teenager, he worked as a missionary to the Indians.

Next to the Bible, Johnny's favorite book was *Aesop's Fables*. The tales of the animals and their human behavior captured his imagination, and he tried to live the lessons taught by the stories.

Sometimes Johnny had mystical, mysterious visions in which angels would appear to him. When he was about twenty-six years old, an angel told Johnny Chapman to plant apple trees in the wilderness so that settlers moving west could enjoy their fruit.

Johnny began collecting apple seeds from cider mills in western Pennsylvania. He carried them in a giant leather sack, which he slung over his back. He also carried a few small pouches of seeds in his pockets to give to people he met. He did most of his planting in Ohio and Indiana, hiking hundreds of miles year 'round.

There's no doubt about it—Johnny Appleseed was an unusual man. He was thin and wiry, and rarely shaved or cut his hair. He wore whatever old clothes people would trade him for his seeds, but usually he wore a sauce-pot on his head and a coffee sack with arm holes cut out of it as a shirt.

Sometimes someone would give him a pair of shoes, but as soon as Johnny came upon a needy fellow, he would gladly give them up. Johnny loved to feel the earth between his toes.

As Johnny made his way across the land, he would clear a field in the wilderness and plant his seeds. Then he would build a fence around the seedlings and move on. Settlers heading through the countryside would find Johnny's orchards and feel at home. Families moving west would dig up some trees to replant on their homesteads.

Johnny would visit each cabin he passed, helping with the chores, spreading the latest news, and amusing the children with songs and stories. He also started what may have been the first lending library on the frontier. Along with his seeds, Johnny carried religious books. He would leave a few pages at each home and collect them when he passed by again.

Johnny realized that he could learn much from the Indians. His strange appearance, his knowledge of the deep woods, and the fact that he carried no weapons won him the admiration of the Indians. They considered him a medicine man who had magical powers. He learned their languages and how to use herbs to heal injuries. He spent as much time with the Indians as with the settlers.

During a visit with the Indians, Johnny learned that they were planning to kill the settlers whose cabins dotted the forest. Johnny spent the night racing through the woods, dressed in his coffee sack, knocking on every cabin door.

To each sleepy settler he shouted, "The spirit of the Lord is upon me and He has anointed me to blow the trumpet in the wilderness and sound an alarm in the forest! The Indians are at your doors!" Hearing the warning, the settlers were able to escape danger.

Another time, the Indians were closing in on a white settlement, and the settlers' only hope was to get a message to a fort thirty miles away. But the settlers knew that any messenger would probably be killed. Even so, Johnny Appleseed volunteered for the duty. He was able to make it safely over the trails he knew so well. Troops were sent from the fort and the families in the settlement were saved.

It wasn't just human life that Johnny considered to be precious. To him, every living thing had an equal right to be alive. He never ate meat, and he was as courteous to animals as he was to people.

During a howling winter snowstorm, Johnny sought shelter in a hollow log. As he climbed in, he noticed that the log was already occupied by a hibernating bear. Rather than push the groggy bear out, Johnny risked his own life by sleeping outside in the freezing cold, huddled next to the log.

Johnny's love of animals even extended to insects. A hornet once flew into his clothes. As he tried to shake it loose, it stung him several times. When asked why he didn't kill it, he replied, "Why should I kill it? It's only behaving the way God intended it to behave."

Another time Johnny smothered his campfire the moment he noticed that bugs were being drawn into it and burned.

Johnny Appleseed planted trees and protected animals for almost fifty years. He died near Fort Wayne, Indiana, after devoting his life to spreading kindness across the rough frontier.

How Brer Rabbit Tricked Brer Fox

It's a fact of nature that foxes and rabbits don't get along. Brer Rabbit and Brer Fox were no different. They pretended to be cordial, but they couldn't resist playing terrible tricks on each other.

One fine day, Brer Fox was enjoying a glass of lemonade with his friend Miss Meadows. They sat in the shade, sipping their drinks and watching butterflies in Miss Meadows's magnolia tree. Brer Fox entertained Miss Meadows with a story about how he had tricked Brer Rabbit into getting hopelessly tangled in a big, sticky glob of tar.

Miss Meadows loved the story so much that she told it to all her neighbors. A few days later, Brer Rabbit paid a call on Miss Meadows. She was playing croquet with a group of her friends. When they saw Brer Rabbit coming, they teased him about the tar without mercy.

Brer Rabbit stayed cool as a cucumber. He said "Ladies, Brer Fox may think he's very clever, but he's really not so bright. He's got no more brains than a riding horse. In fact, my father used to ride him like a horse years ago. That's all Brer Fox will ever be to me—a riding horse."

Saying that, Brer Rabbit stood up, adjusted his jacket and derby, and strutted home.

When Brer Fox heard what Brer Rabbit was saying about him, he seethed with anger. He marched over to Miss Meadows's house and said through clenched teeth, "I don't deny that I worked for Brer Rabbit's father. But sure as I'm standing here, I'll make Brer Rabbit chew up his words and spit them out where you can see them. You just wait." He turned and stormed off.

Brer Fox was determined to pay Brer Rabbit back for the humiliation he had caused. He mulled over one plan after another, and figured that whatever trick he played, it had to be in front of Miss Meadows and her neighbors. The first step was to get Brer Rabbit to Miss Meadows's house.

Brer Fox headed straight for Brer Rabbit's house. He knocked on Brer Rabbit's door. No answer. He knocked louder. No answer. He pounded again—Blam! Blam! Blam!

From inside came Brer Rabbit's voice: "Is that you, Brer Fox?" he said weakly. "I'm mighty sick. Please send a doctor."

"I come to tell you that Miss Meadows is having a garden party," said Brer Fox in a sickeningly sweet voice. "I told her I'd fetch you. Come along. It'll surely make you feel better."

"No, I'm too sick," replied Brer Rabbit. "I can't walk all the way to Miss Meadows's house."

"It won't be much of a party without you," pleaded Brer Fox. "How 'bout if I carry you there?"

"But how do you intend to carry me, Brer Fox?" asked Brer Rabbit.

"In my arms," answered Brer Fox.

"Oh, no. Absolutely not. I'm afraid you'll drop me," said Brer Rabbit. "How 'bout carrying me on your back?"

"Well, fine," agreed Brer Fox. "I'll carry you on my back."

"But I can't ride without a saddle," declared Brer Rabbit.

"I'll get you a saddle," replied Brer Fox.

Brer Fox would do anything to get Brer Rabbit to Miss Meadows's house so he could embarrass him.

"A saddle's not much good without a bridle," observed Brer Rabbit.

"Well then, I guess I'll get a bridle, too," said Brer Fox.

"And don't forget blinders. I don't want you getting startled and throwing me off," added Brer Rabbit, "I'm feeling poorly enough as it is."

"Fine, fine," responded Brer Fox. "I'll get all the things you ask, and I'll carry you almost the whole way to Miss Meadows's house. But you have to get down and walk the rest of the way."

"Agreed!" said Brer Rabbit.

A short while later, Brer Fox trotted up to Brer Rabbit's house wearing a saddle, a bridle, and blinders. He looked like a circus pony.

Brer Rabbit, wearing an elegant velvet jacket, silk trousers and vest, and a top hat, hopped into the saddle. "Let's get to that party," he said to Brer Fox, and the two set off for Miss Meadows's.

By and by, Brer Fox felt Brer Rabbit lift his left leg.

"What'cha doin' up there, Brer Rabbit?" he asked.

"Just adjusting my cuff, Brer Fox," Brer Rabbit replied.

They headed further down the road when Brer Fox felt Brer Rabbit lift his right leg.

"Now why are you fidgeting?" he asked.

"I'm just shortenin' the stirrup," was Brer Rabbit's answer.

Brer Rabbit was actually putting on spurs. He knew that Brer Fox had some trick planned for him when they got to Miss Meadows's house. Brer Rabbit was determined to act first.

The two trotted along without further fuss, and soon they were around the corner from Miss Meadows's house. "Here's where you get off, Brer Rabbit," said Brer Fox.

"I think not, Brer Fox," declared Brer Rabbit as he dug his spurs into Brer Fox's sides.

Like a shot, Brer Fox lunged ahead. Brer Rabbit rode him like a jockey right into Miss Meadows's yard, where all the neighbors were gathered. Brer Rabbit tipped his hat to Miss Meadows, steered Brer Fox over to the fence, and hitched him to a post.

"Ladies," said Brer Rabbit, smiling with glee, "didn't I tell you Brer Fox was my family's riding horse? He's not all he used to be, but he still manages to get around."

John Henry

John Henry was a mountain of a man. He stood close to seven feet tall and had shoulders as broad as a door.

He was born on a plantation in Alabama, and everyone knew he was the fastest, strongest, hardest-working man in the whole state. He could pick more cotton quicker, clean it better, and tote more bales farther than anyone.

One day the overseer of the plantation took John Henry aside and said to him:

"John, you know there's talk of President Lincoln freeing the slaves. I just want to let you know that when that day comes, there'll still be work to do on the plantation. You and your wife Polly Ann will always be welcome to stay on. I'll pay you a fair wage."

To this, John Henry replied:

"You've been more than fair. But there's a lot of world out there I ain't seen and a lot of jobs that need doin'. I 'preciate your generosity, but if President Lincoln frees the slaves, I believe I want to wander 'round and see what this country's all about."

Not long after that conversation, the slaves were freed. John Henry and Polly Ann left the plantation and traveled from place to place doing odd jobs. John never felt comfortable anywhere for any length of time.

John heard that there was work to be done on the Mississippi, and so they set off. The sight of the river brought chills of excitement to John Henry and Polly Ann. Never had they seen a river so wide or a ship as big as a genuine Mississippi riverboat.

John was hired on the spot as a deck hand. He loved working on the river, loading and unloading logs, grain, and cotton. He could lift more cargo, move it quicker, and stack it higher than anyone else on the Mississippi.

But soon even life on the river lost its magic for John.

"You know," John said to Polly Ann when he returned home one evening, "there's something I'm looking for, but I don't know what it is. I've worked at plenty of jobs since leavin' the plantation, but none of 'em hold my interest very long."

"John Henry," replied Polly Ann, "you're a man with a mission. Some men are born to the easy life, but you know you can't be happy unless you're hard at work. You just gotta find that job that you've been put on this earth to do. And wherever you go lookin', I'll be right beside you."

"You're right, sugar pie," said John, bending way down to give his wife a kiss. "Tomorrow's a new day. Maybe I'll find where I'll be happy."

It was time for John Henry and Polly Ann to move on.

Their travels took them to the hills of West Virginia, and that's where John Henry found his life's mission. The answer came clear as a bell. It was the ring of hammer against stone as work crews laid tracks for the B&O Railroad. Railroads were something new, and thousands of miles of track had to be put down, ties needed cutting, and tunnels needed digging and blasting.

To John Henry, the ring of the steel rails was the sound of his future.

"Polly Ann," he declared, "I'm gonna be a steel-drivin' man!"

The pick and shovel felt natural in John Henry's enormous hands as soon as he picked them up. Each day he would leap out of bed at the crack of dawn, grab his tools, and head to the worksite. He'd work from sunup to sundown, driving steel rods into solid rock so that the land could be leveled and the Big Bend Tunnel could be built. John Henry could drive more steel deeper and quicker than anybody else.

Each strike of John Henry's twenty-pound hammer made a shower of sparks that lit the sky. The ringing could be heard for miles. As he worked the rock, John Henry would sing:

> *This mighty country's mighty vast*
> *And full of mighty chores,*
> *But I can work 'em mighty fast*
> *And holler out for more.*
>
> *A life of work I do respect*
> *I ain't got no complaints*
> *'Cause the workin' man, I do suspect*
> *Is second to the saints.*
>
> *Some men can't wait for the noontime break*
> *But me, I work right through it,*
> *'Cause work for me's a piece of cake*
> *And I love to get down to it.*
>
> *So as my hammer bites the ground*
> *Just listen to it ringing!*
> *I am the proudest man around*
> *Hear the words I'm singing!*

One day, just like any other day, John Henry was hammering and singing, singing and hammering, when a strange noise broke his concentration.

It started out as a low chug-chug, but John Henry knew it couldn't be a train because the track hadn't been laid yet. As the sound got closer, he started to hear a thud-thud-thud. Then added to the chug-chug and the thud-thud-thud came a hiss-crunch-ding, hiss-crunch-ding.

The sound grew louder—chug-chug thud-thud-thud hiss-crunch-ding! Everyone dropped his hammer and looked to see where the awful noise was coming from.

Over the hill rose a gleaming silver machine driven by an oily-looking man in a shiny suit. Every railroad man looked on, wide-eyed and open-mouthed, as the stranger drove that chugging, thudding, hissing machine right up to the foreman's office and parked it. The contraption gave a quick chug and a gasp, and then was silent.

The driver hopped down in front of the foreman. As he pushed a business card into the foreman's hand, he chirped, "Allow me to introduce myself. I'm Chuck Geary, and I'm here to sell you this fine machine."

"But what's it do?" asked the foreman.

"Do? Why it does the work of five men," piped Chuck Geary. "This here's a steam drill. It digs through stone—any stone—and drives steel. It's easy to operate. It's fast. And," added Geary with a wink, "it don't get tired or sick or need breaks."

"We got something just like that," said the foreman, poking the card into Geary's handkerchief pocket. "Only he's no machine. His name's John Henry."

"Well," said Geary, "Tell you what. Why don't you pit your man Henry against this here steam drill. If the drill digs a deeper hole, you'll buy it. If Henry's hole is deeper, I'll pay you the price of the machine."

Hearing this, John Henry stepped forward: "Take the challenge, boss. You've been watching me drive steel for three years. You know what I can do. I can beat any machine, for sure."

"Geary," said the foreman, "I believe in my man John Henry. I accept your wager."

The railroad men, who had been watching breathlessly all the while, let loose with cheers and applause for John Henry.

A day for the contest was picked, and the rules were laid down. John Henry and the machine were to work on the side of Big Bend Mountain. They were to work for eight hours. At the end of that time, whoever dug the deeper hole would be declared the winner.

The whole town turned out before sunrise to see the contest. They brought picnic baskets and folding chairs, and they dressed in their best Sunday clothes.

John Henry and Chuck Geary met in front of the mountain and shook hands.

"Take your places, gentlemen," called the foreman.

John Henry walked to his place at the side of the mountain and picked up one of the two new sledgehammers that Polly Ann had given him the night before. Chuck Geary hopped into his steam drill and started the hissing, grinding engine.

"Gentlemen . . . begin!" shouted the foreman, firing a gun into the air.

The steam drill roared to life and attacked the mountain with screaming power.

John Henry tore into the hill just as fiercely, his hammer flashing in the morning's first sunbeams. Sparks flew. The steel rods sang. The folks cheered John on.

Geary's steam drill chewed into the earth. It shrieked and squealed and spat rock as it inched its way in.

John Henry, shirtless and covered with dust and sweat, was smiling as he flung his hammer repeatedly into the stone.

And so it went, hour after hour. John Henry kept up with Geary inch for inch. After the fifth hour, Geary began to pull ahead. Six inches. Eight inches. A foot and more.

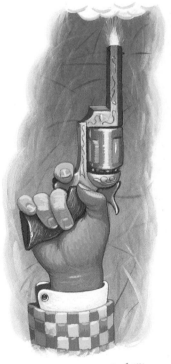

John Henry could hear his opponent's success as the machine bored into the hill. He could feel the tension in the crowd as he began to fall behind.

Then, with a clang, the drill stopped turning. Geary had to make a repair. John seized the opportunity. He grabbed his second sledge, and with a hammer in each hand, he fought that mountain like it was the devil himself. Left-right, left-right, he smashed and crunched and shattered the rock 'til you'd think those hammers would be red-hot.

Geary finally repaired his machine, but John Henry had pulled ahead. There was less than an hour to go. Could Geary make up for lost time? He'd sure try.

Meanwhile John Henry kept doing what he did best—the job he knew he was put on this earth to do. But he was mighty tired, and he was starting to show it.

The minutes ticked by. Inch by inch Geary closed the lead.

Then they were down to the last minute of the contest.

The crowd started counting: "Fifty-nine, fifty-eight . . ."

John Henry thought, "I got to do this."

". . . forty-five, forty-four . . ."

Chuck Geary thought, "I got him on the run."

". . . twenty-six, twenty-five . . ."

"A man can do more than a machine," thought John Henry as he mustered his last bit of strength to get his final strokes in.

Geary poured on a dangerous amount of steam. The drill threatened to shake apart as it cut into the rock. "No man can lick this machine," muttered Geary.

". . . three, two, one, TIME!" screamed the crowd.

John Henry stepped away from the mountain. Geary cut his engine. The crowd was silent.

The foreman measured Geary's tunnel. "Twelve feet, eight inches," he announced.

He walked over to see John Henry's work: "Fourteen feet, two inches!"

The crowd went wild. Polly Ann rushed to John Henry and gave him a big kiss. John smiled, and then collapsed. He died right there, still holding the hammers.

Some say John Henry worked himself to death. Others say he died when he realized that the machines would eventually win and men like him wouldn't be needed anymore. But John Henry died doing what he loved best.

Davy Crockett

Many wonderful things have been said about Davy Crockett. Some of them are even true.

Some folks say that he could speak the language of the animals, and that he could whip his weight in wildcats. Some even believe that he was half alligator and half horse!

The truth is that Davy Crockett was an ordinary man who fought for what he believed. He's an important figure in American history, but he was such a colorful character that people couldn't help making up exaggerated stories about him.

Davy was born in the mountains of Tennessee in 1786. He didn't have an easy boyhood. When he was about twelve years old, Davy's father had to hire him out to help drive cattle to earn money. He traveled four hundred miles on foot and then had to find his way back home. When he returned, his father promised he would never hire him out again. A few years later, Davy's father owed his neighbors some money, and Davy volunteered to work off the debts.

When Davy wasn't working or learning to read and write, he spent his time tracking and hunting. He was a first-class shot and could move through the forest without making a sound.

Some folks say that Davy was hunting one day when he spotted a raccoon in a tree. As Davy carefully took aim, the raccoon said "Wait a minute—you're Davy Crockett, ain't you?"

Davy proudly admitted that he was.

"Then you needn't bother firing," said the raccoon. "I surrender."

Of course, Davy had to let the critter go free after that.

Other folks say that's not the way it happened at all. They reckon that it was Davy's big, bright grin and winning personality that helped him bag the raccoon. Davy just had to smile and the raccoon fell out of the tree right into Davy's game pouch.

No matter which story you like better it was true that people everywhere knew about Davy's hunting skills. Wherever he went, he was challenged to shooting contests. He grew tired of these competitions, so he thought of a way of putting an end to them while keeping his reputation as a sharpshooter.

During his last contest, Davy fired two shots. The first hit the bull's-eye exactly in the middle. For the second shot, Davy missed the target on purpose. When he went to inspect the target, he secretly stuck a spent bullet into the hole made by the first bullet.

"Two perfect bull's-eyes," announced Davy. And sure enough, when the challenger inspected the target, he found two slugs occupying the same hole. After that, Davy wasn't challenged again.

In 1806, when Davy was twenty years old, he married Polly Finley. They had two sons, and eventually moved deeper into the Tennessee hills, where game was plenty and neighbors were scarce.

But as the Crocketts moved into the woods, they moved closer to hostile Indian country. Davy went to join the militia that organized to fight the Red Stick Indians, who had murdered hundreds of white settlers. Davy's skill in shooting and tracking served the militia well, and the Red Sticks were scared away.

Davy returned home to Polly. They had a daughter, but then Polly died. Shortly afterward, Davy married a widow whose husband had died during a battle against the Red Sticks.

Davy and his new family moved to Lawrence County, Tennessee, where Davy ran a gunpowder mill and a gristmill. His neighbors elected him colonel of the militia, and later he became commissioner of the growing town of Lawrenceburg. His popularity as a politician and as a bear-hunter grew. People persuaded him to run for the state legislature.

People flocked to hear Davy's speeches. He appealed to the plain folks of Tennessee because he was one of them. His speeches weren't full of puffery and promises. Rather than trying to make himself look important, Davy would poke fun at himself. Once, when he couldn't think of anything to talk about, he told his audience that he felt like a man trying to get cider out of an empty barrel. He said he used to have good speeches in him, but he had used them up.

More often, Davy would let his competitor speak himself hoarse, knowing that the audience would grow tired of hearing about the government. When it was Davy's turn to speak, he would tell a short, funny story and send everyone home.

Davy won the election and represented the people of his county in the Tennessee legislature. As the voice of the settlers, he argued that they should have the right to buy the land they cleared at a fair price.

In his leather breeches and jacket, Davy stood out from the other legislators, who wore suits. At first he was treated like a bumpkin, but he soon won everyone's respect with his good sense and humor.

While Davy was in the legislature, a flood destroyed his mills. When his term was up, he decided to give up politics and rebuild what he had lost. But that wasn't how things turned out.

One day, a newspaper announced that Davy was running for a second term in the legislature. The announcement was a joke, but Davy turned the joke on the joker—he ran for another term.

By now his reputation as a political hero was legendary. For his campaign, he wore a buckskin jacket with two large pockets in it. One pocket held a pint of whiskey; the other held tobacco. People liked to chew tobacco in those days, and in Tennessee, folks were proud of their whiskey. Davy courted voters by telling stories and offering them a sip of his whiskey. The voter would have to spit out his tobacco before he could take a sip, but Davy would replace it with fresh tobacco when he was done with his story. The voter would be no worse off than he was before—in fact, he'd be happier. Davy won the election and represented ten Tennessee counties.

When Davy wasn't in the legislature, he thought of starting a business making and selling wooden barrel parts. These were in demand in New Orleans, but in order to get them there, Davy had to sail them down the Mississippi River. Davy didn't know much about river navigation—and neither did the captain he hired.

The boats they used were impossible to control in the quick waters of the Mississippi. They ran into a pile of floating logs and began to sink. Davy was trapped inside one boat, but he was able to poke his head through a small opening to keep from drowning. His crew members rushed to help him and saved his life.

Davy returned home, where he was persuaded to run for Congress. Davy lost the first election, but he learned a lot during the campaign and decided to run again.

In the second election, Davy ran against two men who didn't take him seriously. In their speeches, they never even mentioned Davy Crockett's name. During one of these speeches, a flock of guinea hens was crossing nearby, cackling loudly. The speaker became irritated and asked that the birds be driven away.

Davy jumped onto the podium and congratulated the speaker for understanding the language of the birds. "You've ignored me this whole campaign," said Davy, "and now, when my friends the birds come by, shouting 'Crockett, Crockett, Crockett,' you shoo them away."

The audience cheered with approval. Davy won the election and became Congressman Crockett.

When Davy joined Congress, the congressmen were considering taking back some of the land that the United States had promised to the Indians. Davy argued fiercely against the plan. He believed the land rightfully belonged to the Indians.

Davy's views made him unpopular, but Davy took it in stride. He told his wife he was sticking up for what was right, not for what would make him popular.

Even Davy Crockett couldn't change the public's mind. The bill was passed, and the Indians lost more of their land. Davy gave up politics and moved to Texas.

Texas was a part of Mexico, but many American settlers made their homes there. As more settlers came to Texas, the angrier the Mexican government became. Mexico wanted to keep its control of Texas, but the Texans wanted Texas to be part of the United States.

War was in the air, and Davy Crockett agreed to fight for the independence of Texas. When Davy heard that Mexico was sending troops toward a fortress in San Antonio called the Alamo, he rushed to help protect the fort. Davy tried to gather as many men as he could to fight the Mexican army at the Alamo, but few volunteered.

In 1846, four thousand Mexican soldiers attacked the Alamo, which was heroically defended by fewer than two hundred Americans. Even though the Texans were outnumbered, they held off the Mexican army for thirteen days. All the defenders, including Davy Crockett, were killed in the battle for independence.

Throughout his life, Davy Crockett acted for what he believed in, even when the odds were against him, or his beliefs made him unpopular. Through his determination, Davy rose from frontiersman to congressman to hero.

In his life story, Davy wrote:

"I leave this rule for others when I'm dead,
Be always sure you're right—
THEN GO AHEAD!"

The Story of
Bobcat and Coyote

The Native American storytellers of the Great Plains know that long before people were created, the earth was ruled by the animals. There were blue jays, and moles, and turkeys, and porcupines, and most of the other animals we know today, plus a few others you can't find anymore. But these ancient animals weren't ordinary beasts. They had magic in them, and they behaved (and misbehaved) like people.

Coyote was the most magical of the animals. Sometimes he would use his powers for good, as when he created the world and humans from lumps of mud. But mostly Coyote was a trickster who would try to cause trouble for others and end up getting into trouble himself. That's exactly what happened when he played a joke on Bobcat.

When Coyote created the world, he wanted to make it perfect, so he made most of the animals look just like himself. Back then, Coyote didn't look like the coyotes you see today. The original Coyote had silky soft fur of golden brown; a short and slender tail; clear, sparkling eyes; graceful legs; and small, rounded ears. That's also the way the original Bobcat looked.

Coyote and Bobcat were friends. They spent a lot of time on the plains together, hunting and playing through the night. One morning, Coyote woke up early and went to visit Bobcat, but when he arrived, Bobcat was still asleep.

Coyote was about to wake him when a devilish thought crossed his mind.

"Bobcat is too handsome," thought Coyote. "I've given him too much of my good looks. Now's my chance to make some adjustments."

Coyote sang a lullaby into Bobcat's ear to put him into a deep, deep sleep. Then he went to work making Bobcat less handsome.

First he pushed in Bobcat's face, making his muzzle shorter. Then he tugged on Bobcat's ears, making them pointy.

"Oh! Much better than expected!" chuckled Coyote. "But there's more to do."

He shortened Bobcat's legs and stretched his paws; he bobbed his tail and yanked on the corners of his eyes. As he surveyed his progress, Coyote nearly burst with laughter.

"And now—ha, ha!—and now, the final touch!" said Coyote. He scooped up a pawful of pebbles and dust, and sprinkled it onto Bobcat's back.

"Polka dots!" Coyote howled with glee.

All this hilarity exhausted Coyote, so he went to take a nap, giggling all the way home.

A while later, Bobcat woke up.

"What a wonderful rest I've had!" he exclaimed. "I feel brand-new."

He went to the creek for a sip of water. As he leaned over the bank, he saw his reflection.

"Yikes!" he yelped as he jumped back. "What was that creature? It's so ugly! I'll get a drink further upstream."

Bobcat picked a new spot in the creek, but once again he mistook his reflection for a strange animal. "This thing is following me. It must be some kind of fish."

Wherever Bobcat peeked over the bank of the creek, the ugly face peeked back. Finally he gave up and headed home. On the way he passed several of his friends. He was eager to tell them about what he saw in the creek, but they all ran away.

"What's wrong with everyone?" shouted Bobcat. "You'd think I was . . ."

At that moment, Bobcat realized what had happened. He ran back to the creek. "That's me!" he cried. "This has to be the work of Coyote. Just wait until I get my big, ugly paws on him!"

Bobcat ran to Coyote's house. Coyote was sound asleep.

"Well, well," thought Bobcat. "I'll show him what a muzzle should look like," he said as he stretched Coyote's nose and mouth.

"And I'll teach him about pointy ears," he growled, tugging Coyote's ears out of shape.

"How's this for a tail, Coyote?" laughed Bobcat as he stretched Coyote's tail and brushed the fur into a ragged bundle.

"And what about those legs?" he said, pulling them to twice their length.

"Let's not forget your fur," squealed Bobcat, trying to catch his breath because he was laughing so hard. He picked up some soot and rubbed it over Coyote's back, making the fur dark and coarse.

When he was done, Bobcat rolled on the floor, giddy with laughter. "That's the funniest thing I've ever seen!" he bellowed.

Bobcat went back home feeling very proud of himself. But the feeling didn't last. He regretted losing his old friend. He knew he could never forgive Coyote for what Coyote did to him, and he knew that Coyote would never forgive him for taking his revenge. This is how coyotes and bobcats came to look as they do—and why they still don't get along today.

Pocahontas

The Indian princess Pocahontas was eleven years old when she first saw a white man. His name was Captain John Smith, and what a strange sight he was!

Pocahontas, who wore a simple buckskin dress, was amazed by all the layers of clothing the white man wore. "They probably protect his pale skin," she thought, "but how can he move in such things?"

But more than the clothes, what really fascinated Pocahontas were Captain Smith's eyes—they were blue as the sky. What magic was this? What world could he have come from? The curious young princess had to find out.

Captain Smith was one of a hundred men who sailed three ships to America from England in 1611. They were coming to America to look for gold and to settle the land. They came ashore in the Chesapeake Bay. They called the land Virginia, and they called their settlement Jamestown.

But the Englishmen weren't the first people to see this place. The Algonquin Indians had hunted, farmed, and fished there for generations before the strangers discovered it. The Indians felt they had a sacred right to the place the white men called Virginia. They were not going to give it up without a fight.

Pocahontas's father, Powhatan, was the powerful chief of the Algonquins. Of his many children, Pocahontas held a special place in his heart. Pocahontas' real name was Matoak. "Pocahontas" was a nickname her father gave her. It meant "mischievous one."

While the other children of the tribe gathered berries, cleaned animal pelts, and performed other chores, Pocahontas was allowed to dance around the fields and string flowers into necklaces. Sometimes she would forget she was a princess and pretend to be a forest spirit. She would paint scary shapes on her body and make a fearsome headdress of twigs and leaves. She would hide among the trees, waiting for someone from the tribe to pass by. When they did, she would jump out and shriek, trying to frighten them.

When Pocahontas wasn't playing outdoors, she would spend time with her father while he discussed important matters with the medicine men and other tribe advisors.

Powhatan and his advisors were upset about the white men who had come to the bay. They had heard tales of these men, with their deadly thunder sticks and their strange ways. It was said that a thunder stick could kill a brave without even touching him.

"These are powerful sorcerers who come from the edge of the world," said one of Powhatan's advisors.

"This sounds like trouble to me," said another. "I think they mean to take our land."

Powhatan sent for a brave and said: "Go see these white men. Tell them they may rest awhile, or hunt for food, or trade with us, but let them know they are not welcome to stay here."

But the white men did stay. Powhatan didn't chase them away because he feared their magic and also because the strangers brought so many beautiful beads and useful tools to trade.

One day the Indian village buzzed with excitement. A white man had ventured too far from camp and been captured by the Indians. Now he was being brought before Chief Powhatan, who would decide whether he would live or die.

Gossip about the white man spread through the village.

"I heard he's ten feet tall," said one Indian.

"I was told he can make flames fly from his fingertips," whispered another.

This talk went on, each story more silly than the last. Then finally the braves arrived with the prisoner, Captain John Smith.

A hush filled the village. Even the breeze dared not blow.

Captain Smith was brought to Chief Powhatan's longhouse. To Powhatan's left was Pocahontas, who couldn't stop looking at Captain Smith's red hair and blue eyes. To Powhatan's right were his advisors. All around were brightly painted medicine men. No one said a word. Powhatan stared at Smith. Smith stared at Powhatan. Pocahontas held her breath and tried to swallow a nervous giggle.

Captain Smith suddenly spoke the Indian word for greetings.

"He does not seem afraid of my father," thought Pocahontas. "But Powhatan doesnot look pleased."

Using sign language and a few Indian words he had learned, Captain Smith tried to persuade Powhatan that the white settlers meant no harm. Then he offered his compass to the mightly chief. Powhatan inspected it closely, turning it around in his hand. He had never seen a compass, and he couldn't understand why the needle always pointed in the same direction. He was even more puzzled when he tried to touch the needle. A piece of ice was in the way, but the ice was warm and it wouldn't melt! Powhatan had never seen glass before. He didn't know what to make of it.

Pocahontas was spellbound. What other magic could this white man do? She decided she liked Captain Smith. He didn't seem evil to her.

Powhatan and his advisors didn't see things that way. They believed that Smith should be killed at once. The chief ordered two flat boulders to be brought to the longhouse. Captain Smith was forced to kneel on the ground with his head resting on one of the stones. His hands were tied behind his back. He closed his eyes.

"Please father," asked Pocahontas bravely, "spare his life. Perhaps he can teach us wonderful things."

Powhatan refused his daughter's request. He ordered a brave to lift the remaining stone high above Captain Smith's head.

There was only one thing Pocahontas could do—and it was a very serious matter.

"No!" she cried. She leapt up and put her head above Captain Smith's.

Everyone gasped. After a tense moment, Powhatan signaled the brave to put the stone back on the ground. By throwing herself under the boulder,

Pocahontas had done more than save Captain Smith's life. According to Algonquin tradition, she also adopted him as her brother and made him a member of the tribe!

Soon after, Pocahontas and John Smith became great friends. John Smith brought Pocahontas beautiful baubles and beads, and thrilled her with stories of London's wide streets, big buildings, and elegant shops. Together, they learned each other's languages.

Pocahontas also helped Captain Smith by persuading her father to give the settlers corn and meat, since the Englishmen were having trouble establishing the colony. Many of the settlers were ill, and most of them seemed more interested in hunting for gold than for food. Without Pocahontas to soften her father's heart, the colonists would have certainly starved.

More ships came to Jamestown from England. One of them carried gifts to Powhatan from the king of England. These gifts included a big brass bed, a velvet robe, and a crown. But Powhatan was not pleased. He refused to lower his head so the crown could be put on.

"The king of the Algonquins bows to no one," he bellowed. He saw the gifts as a sign that the white men were getting too comfortable in Jamestown, and that they meant to stay. Powhatan decided to stop giving them food, hoping that they would leave.

That winter was difficult for the settlers. Their corn supply had been devoured by rats, and Powhatan sent no aid. He forbade Pocahontas, who was now thirteen, from visiting Jamestown and her white brother. The future looked bleak for the settlers. Then one day, John Smith received an invitation to see Powhatan and discuss arranging a trade. Smith was happy to go, but he was also a little suspicious. Why had the chief changed his mind? "Well," thought Smith, "it will be good to see Pocahontas again."

When Captain Smith arrived, Powhatan did not seem happy to see him. "I have no food to give you," said the chief. "It has been a bad year."

Smith and Powhatan argued into the night, and then Powhatan invited the captain to stay until morning in his cabin in the woods. John Smith really had no choice since it was dangerous to travel at night. He went to the cabin, wondering why he hadn't seen Pocahontas all day. He also wondered why Powhatan had called for him when the chief had nothing to offer.

In the middle of the night, John Smith heard a knock on the cabin door. It was Pocahontas. She had sneaked through the dark and freezing forest to warn Captain Smith that Powhatan planned to kill him that night.

"Once again you have saved my life, dear princess," said John Smith. "All I have to offer you are these beads."

"I cannot take your gift," replied Pocahontas with tears in her eyes. "If my father sees them, he'll know I acted against him. The penalty for that is death."

Pocahontas disappeared into the black night, and John Smith cautiously found his way back to Jamestown.

That was the last Pocahontas saw of John Smith for many years. A few months after she saved his life in the woods, she heard that he was killed when his gunpowder pouch exploded.

Jamestown began to grow as new settlers arrived. This only angered Powhatan, who declared war on the little colony. Pocahontas heard terrible tales of cruelty on both sides. She admired the bravery of the settlers and considered them to be her friends. Secretly she did all she could to help them.

Powhatan did not want his daughter to have anything to do with the white settlers, so he sent her to live with a neighboring Indian village. These Indians, the Potomacs, were ruled by Chief Japazaws. Japazaws was a friend of the white settlers, so Powhatan knew that his daughter would be safe under his care. But Powhatan gave strict instructions not to let Pocahontas visit Jamestown.

When Pocahontas was seventeen, Chief Japazaws was visited by Captain Samuel Argall from England. The war between the Jamestown settlers and Powhatan had grown bloodier, and Captain Argall came to ask Japazaws for help.

"If we can take Pocahontas to Jamestown," the captain explained, "we can keep her there until Powhatan returns the weapons he stole from us. That would end the war."

"That won't work," replied the Indian chief. "Powhatan would be furious. Besides, you will never get Pocahontas to go."

But Captain Argall had a plan.

The next day, Captain Argall explained to Japazaws, his wife, and Pocahontas what it was like to sail across the ocean. "I know," said Captain Argall, "why don't we go aboard my ship and I'll show you how it works!"

"We would like that very much," said Japazaws.

"I cannot come," said Pocahontas.

"Well, I won't go unless Pocahontas goes," said Japazaws's wife.

"You'll come with me," said the Chief angrily.

"No. Not without my friend, Pocahontas," shouted the Chief's wife.

Japazaws and his wife argued a long time. It wasn't a real argument— it was part of Captain Argall's trick to get Pocahontas aboard the ship.

The plan worked. Pocahontas, seeing that she was the cause of the fuss, finally agreed to board the ship.

The guests toured the ship and were fed a delicious meal. Later, Pocahontas became separated from the chief and his wife. Then she looked overboard and saw Japazaws and his wife sailing back to shore in a canoe. Japazaws's wife was clutching a shiny copper kettle and a basket of beads. These were her payment for helping Captain Argall kidnap Princess Pocahontas!

Pocahontas was taken to Jamestown and treated like a royal guest. The women dressed her in skirts and bonnets and blouses like the ones they wore themselves. She learned English manners. The settlers made her feel at home. She understood that by being in Jamestown, perhaps she was helping to end the war sooner.

Powhatan refused to pay the ransom for his daughter. Instead, he sent some broken weapons and a little corn. So Pocahontas stayed with the settlers. Eventually she fell in love with a farmer named John Rolfe.

John Rolfe treated Pocahontas with great kindness. They wanted to get married, but Pocahontas first wanted to see her father, whom she hadn't seen in more than a year.

John and Pocahontas, who had been given the Christian name Rebecca, stood before Powhatan. The Indian princess assured her father that she was being treated well. Powhatan approved the marriage and promised peace between the settlers and the Indians.

Pocahontas was the first American Indian to marry a white man. Soon they had a baby, Thomas, and the young family traveled to London. London was more wondrous than Pocahontas could have possibly imagined. Along with the Rolfes came an Indian scout who was instructed by Powhatan to count all the white men he saw. The scout put a notch on a stick each time he saw a white man, but after only a short time, he tossed the stick away in frustration. So many white men!

The Indian Princess was clothed in beautiful gowns. She met London's most important people—even the king and queen. Her biggest surprise was meeting her adopted brother, John Smith, who hadn't been killed after all.

The two old friends were glad to see each other, but they were also a little sad. It was as if they were meeting for the first time. No longer was Pocahontas a mischievous little girl in a buckskin dress. Now she was Lady Rebecca, the toast of London. And John Smith was also a celebrity for having helped settle Jamestown.

Pocahontas and John Smith remained dear friends. They had introduced each other to exciting new worlds, and had shared a dream of peace between the American Indians and the Europeans.

Pecos Bill

exas is a darn big state, so it's only right that it should have a hero all its own. That's Pecos Bill, King of the Cowboys.

Bill was born back East, one of thirteen or fifteen, or even twenty kids. These kids were so active it was hard to count them. Since Bill was the youngest of the bunch, most of the hand-me-down toys had been lost or broken, so Bill had to find toys of his own.

Like any baby, Bill wanted a teddy bear. Since there was none in sight, he climbed out of his crib one day and caught himself a genuine grizzly, which he killed with his bare hands and dragged back home.

Bill's parents admired their son's ingenuity, but didn't think keeping a dead bear in the crib was a healthy thing to do. So they made Bill a blanket from the hide and had the rest of the bear for supper that night.

When Bill was still a baby, no more than two or three years old, his mother heard about some folks moving in about fifty miles away.

"Neighborhood's getting crowded, Pa," she said. "Let's head west."

"That's a good idea, Ma," Pa said.

So they loaded their covered wagon and set out for the American wilderness.

Almost every blessed inch of space inside the wagon was filled with one youngster or another, not to mention the pots and pans, the clothes, and all the other belongings people like to take when they move. When the family got to Texas, the wagon hit a whopping bump in the trail. Baby Bill was bounced clear out the back. Problem was, no one noticed for a week, and by then it was too late to look for him. Bill's parents were sad to lose him, but they knew he was tougher than leather and would get along somehow.

As a matter of fact, Bill got along fine. To escape the hot sun, Bill crawled into a nearby cave and promptly fell asleep. It just so happened that this cave was the home of a family of coyotes. The mama coyote took a shine to baby Bill right off and she raised him like one of her own.

Bill learned the ways of the coyotes—hunting, running around, and baying at the moon. He learned the language of all the animals, and was an eloquent speaker. Pretty soon, he forgot his human family and believed himself to be 100 percent coyote.

One day, when he was about twenty years old, Bill was hunched over a bank of the Pecos River, lapping up some water with his tongue, coyote-style, when a cowboy spotted him.

"What in tarnation?" said the cowboy. "You're sippin' water like you was some sorta varmint."

"Ain't you ever seen a coyote before?" asked Bill.

"'Course I have," said the cowboy. "But you ain't no coyote. You're human."

"Am too a coyote," insisted Bill. "Ain't I got fleas like one?"

"Lots o' people got fleas," replied the cowboy. "That don't prove nothin'. If you're a coyote, then where's your tail?"

"Why it's . . . uh . . . oh . . . Well, whatd'ya know!" shouted Bill, who never noticed he didn't have a tail. "I guess I am human after all."

The cowboy put the "Pecos" before Bill's given name, in honor of the river where Bill first learned he was human. He got Bill some decent clothes and invited him to join his gang of cattle ranchers. That sounded fine to Bill, so the two headed off. The cowboy rode his horse, and Bill, who had no horse, walked alongside.

They hadn't gone far when a huge mountain lion leaped out of the sage-brush and landed square on Pecos Bill's back. Without hardly breaking stride, Bill flipped that cat over his shoulders and wrestled it to the ground. The two kicked up a load of dust as they fought it out. Finally Bill had the mountain lion pinned.

"Give up, varmint?" growled Bill, in mountain lion talk.

"I give! I give!" cried the lion.

Bill jumped on the back of the mountain lion. Riding the big cat like a horse, he and the cowboy continued on. They had gone just a few more miles when a ten-foot rattlesnake sprang at them.

Without wasting an instant, Pecos Bill jumped off the mountain lion, grabbed the snake by the rattle, and started swinging it 'round and 'round over his head. As the snake spun, it grew thinner and longer.

When Bill was done, that snake was thirty feet long but no wider than your little finger. All the poison and fight had been swung out of it. Pecos Bill rolled the snake into a coil like a rope and flung it over one shoulder. The cowboy was mighty impressed.

They reached the campsite without any more difficulties. The other cowboys didn't know what to say when they saw Bill riding a mountain lion and wearing a snake over one shoulder. But they could see he was a good man, and he got along well with every one of them.

Pecos Bill followed the cowboys to the range the next day to see what cattle ranching was all about. He was still riding that mountain lion, and the sight of it spooked one of the cows, which started to run away. Bill made a loop at one end of his snake-rope, threw it around the cow's neck, and quickly brought it down.

"Why, I've never seen anything like that, Pecos Bill!" drawled one of the cowboys. "You've just invented cattle roping!"

"Maybe so," said Bill, "but if I'm gonna be a success at this business, I'd better get a real horse."

The cowboys told Bill about a horse called Widow-maker. He was the fastest, most beautiful horse in the world, but he was also the most ornery and impossible to control. Bill knew that this was the horse for him.

Bill found Widow-maker in the mountains. He roped him and rode him for three days, as the horse bucked his way across four states. Finally Widow-maker gave in to Bill. The two became friends and together they rounded up nearly every cow in Texas.

The only time Pecos Bill ever got mad at Widow-maker was when the horse almost cost him his bride, a woman named Slue-foot Sue.

The first time Bill saw Sue, she was riding a giant catfish in the Rio Grande River. Some folks say it was a whale she was riding, but that's an honest mistake. Catfish can grow to the size of whales in the Rio Grande.

Anyway, Slue-foot Sue was riding the back of that fish and yipping with glee. Her riding skill caught Bill's eye, and her beauty stole his heart. The two started courting and before long, they decided to get married.

For the wedding, Slue-foot Sue wore a fancy, store-bought wedding dress with a great big bustle. For her wedding present, she talked Bill into letting her ride Widow-maker. Only Bill forgot to tell Widow-maker in advance, and that horse never let anyone ride him except Bill.

Right after the wedding, Sue ran out of the church and jumped smack-dab onto Widow-maker's back. The surprised horse bucked like all-get-out and sent Slue-foot Sue sailing over the moon. When she finally came back to earth, she landed on her bustle and bounced right up to the moon again.

Down she came and up she went. Up she went and down she came. It took Pecos Bill the better part of two days before he could rope her and keep her on the planet. But finally he succeeded and the two lived happily ever after.